BILLY THE GREAT
Rosa Guy

illustrated by
Caroline Binch

LONDON · VICTOR GOLLANCZ LTD · 1991

For Otonia
R G

For Sam and Sybil
C B

First published in Great Britain 1991
by Victor Gollancz Ltd,
14 Henrietta Street, London WC2E 8QJ

Text © Rosa Guy 1991
Illustrations © Caroline Binch 1991

A catalogue record for this book
is available from the British Library

ISBN 0 575 04284 2

Printed and bound in Singapore by Imago Publishing Ltd

"What a bright little baby," Billy's mother said,
the day he was born. Billy's father agreed.
   Later, when Billy turned his head to look around,
his father said, "See his fine, strong back."
   Billy kicked his legs and grinned.

When Billy was one year old, Mum said, "My Billy is going to be a great man."
Dad said, "Let's give him time to grow a little."
Billy just laughed.

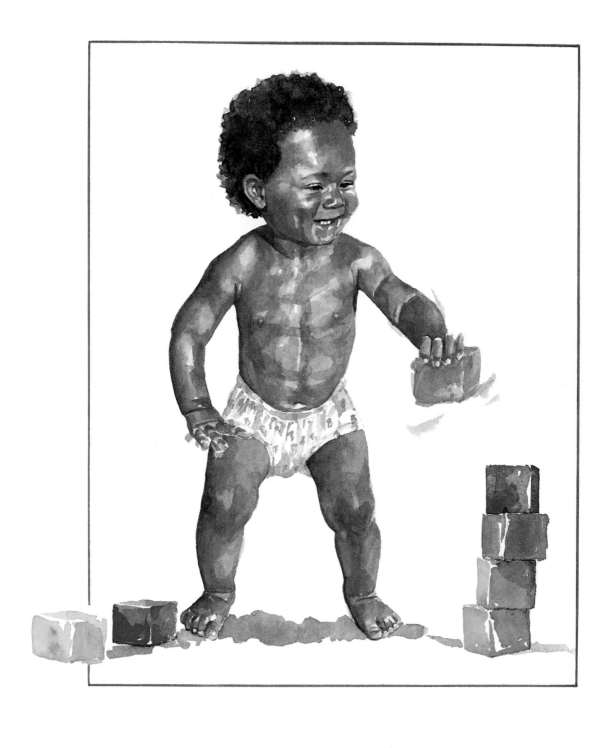

When Billy was four, his mother said, "We have to get Billy ready for college."

"Let's get him through school first," Dad said.

Billy smiled.

"My Billy is going to be a teacher," Mum said, when she saw him teaching his teddy bear the ABC, just the way she had taught Billy. "He might even be a university professor."

"What?" Dad said. "Shut him up in a classroom? With his strong back and legs? No, Billy's going to be a great footballer."

One day Billy bandaged his dog from head to paws, except for his nose. Mum said, "How intelligent. Billy left room for Rover to breathe. My Billy's going to be a doctor."

She bought Billy a stethoscope and more bandages.
But Rover refused to let Billy practise on him again.

When Billy was six, Rodney moved in next door. Rodney's father was a lorry driver. He was a big man, with broad shoulders and thick, tattooed arms. Billy liked Rodney.

"How 'ya doing, kid," Rodney said, looking down at Billy.

"My name is Rodney, but call me Rod."

That made Billy feel grown-up. "How 'ya doing, Rod," he said.

"Come round for tea later," Rod said.

Billy went. He tried to keep up with Rod, eating piece after piece of pie.

He got a tummy-ache. "I don't want you to go to that boy's house again," Mum said. "He's too big for you to play with. Besides, his father has tattoos."

"But I like Rod," Billy said.

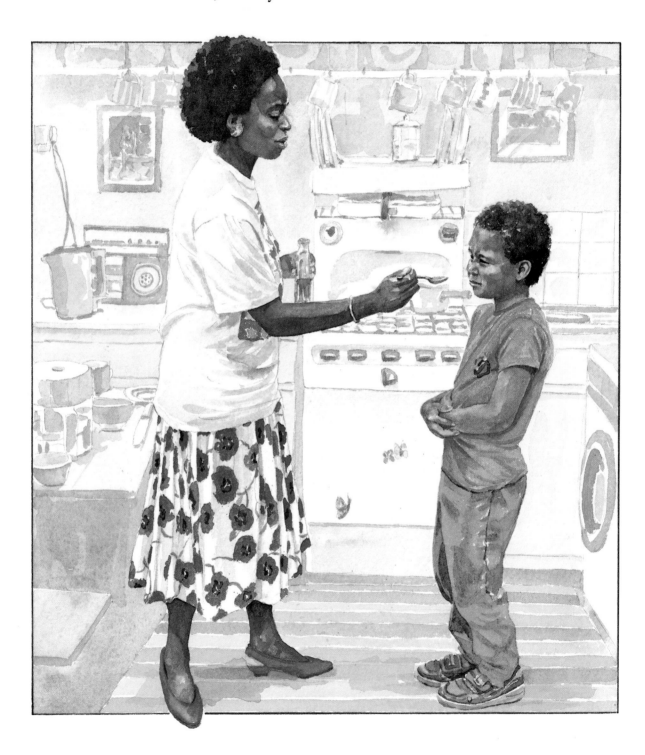

Rod was ten years old. He climbed trees, and ran as fast
as the wind. Billy tried to climb trees too. When Mum saw
him she said, "I don't want you to play with that boy, he's
too old and too rough."

Billy said, "I like Rod. I like climbing trees."

"You'll tear your nice clothes," Mum said. "Go and
play with children your own age."

"I don't want to play with *children*," Billy said, "I want to play with Rod."

Mum said, "Play with children your own age."

"I'll get dirty," Billy said.

"A bit of dirt won't matter," Mum said.

Billy went to play with children his own age. They made
mud pies and threw them at him.

Mud went all over Billy.

Billy threw mud pies back.

Mud got into Jeanie's hair and she ran home crying.

She brought her mum over to Billy's house.
"Billy's sorry," Mum told Jeanie's mother.
"Billy, tell Jeanie you won't do it again."
"She started it," Billy said.
"Now Billy," Mum said, "tell Jeanie you're sorry."
Billy refused. He wasn't sorry.

Then Mum scolded him. "How did you get so dirty?"
she said. "How did you get mud in your hair?"
She scrubbed hard to get him clean. It hurt.

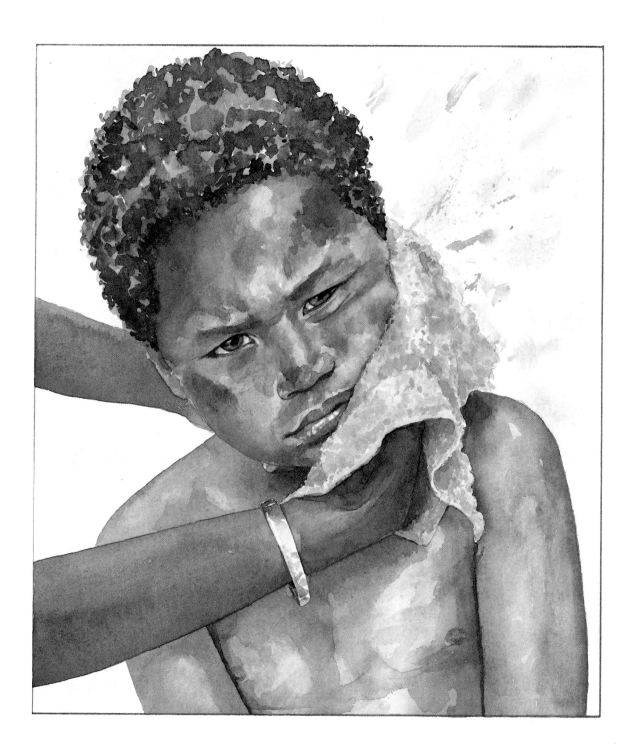

On Billy's seventh birthday, Dad bought Billy a
big leather football.
  "Now we can start training you to be
a great footballer," Dad said.

He took Billy into the garden. "Stand there and watch, Billy," Dad said. "First I'll show you the proper way to kick the ball."

Billy stood and watched. Dad kicked the ball. It flew through the air and bounced off the tree.

The ball flew and flew, and flew right through the glass of Rod's window.

Rod's father came out. He shouted at Dad.
Rod's father was big and broad, and he
had tattoos.
    "Don't shout at me," Dad said.
Then Rod came out.

"How 'ya doing, kid," Rod said.
    "How 'ya doing, Rod," Billy said.
    "I can do handstands and cartwheels,"
Rod said. "Can you?"
    "I think I can," Billy said.

Rod stood on his hands, feet in the air. Then he flipped over on one hand, then on to his feet,

then back on his other hand, just like a wheel.
Billy tried and tried.

On his third try he stood on his hands, his feet in the air.
He flipped over on one hand then stood up. He had done it!
   "Billy!" Mum called from the kitchen. She sounded angry.
Then she saw Rod's father, eye-balling Billy's father.
   "He broke my window," Rod's father said.
   "Did you tell him we'd fix it?" Mum said.
   "He shouted at me," Dad said.

"Mum," Billy said, "Rod showed me how to do a handstand — watch!" Once again Billy stood on his hands, his feet straight out and steady over his head.

Mum stared. . .

"Did you call me for something, Mum?" Billy asked.
    She started to smile.
    "Billy, that's great," she said. "What clever boys
you both are."

Mum smiled at the Dads, too. "Come in and have some tea," she said.

Billy and Rod raced each other and did
cartwheels over the grass.